LOVE
FOR THE
CHILDREN

Joan E. Calliste

ISBN 978-1-63630-453-3 (Paperback)
ISBN 978-1-63630-454-0 (Digital)

Covenant Books, Inc.
11661 Hwy 707
Murrells Inlet, SC 29576
www.covenantbooks.com

CONTENTS

Acknowledgments v

Protecting the Neighbourhood 1
Special Offering..4
I Am Ashamed of You 6
Kindness 8
Finding Our Way 11
Thank God for a Mother's Prayer 13
The Song of a Child Makes a Difference 16
Change through a Dream 18
Ugly Glasses 21
Missionary for Jesus..24
Trust in the Lord Always 26
The Little Preacher 28
Prayer Is the Answer 30
Blessing in Disguise...32
Honesty 35
The Power of Prayer 37
Returning Home 40
Tommy's Birthday 43
The Unseen Lawyer...45
Going Camping 47

ACKNOWLEDGMENTS

This book of children's stories is dedicated to Elder Paula Waterton for her single-minded pursuit in sharing our Lord's message, and for her refusal to allow my dismissive and unbelieving response of "No, I can't do it" stand in her way. It is because of Elder Waterton's determination that I have discovered my God-given talent. As you enjoy God's gift to the author, it is hoped that, when God reveals His gift to you, you will accept and embrace it. Remember that You are God's child, and He loves you.

I also would like to say a special thank you to my loving friend Lorna Moses (deceased), whose constant encouragement has contributed to my present reality.

Dr. Lesliann Boatswain, I thank you for investing your personal time into typing my simple stories—stories that have now changed my life.

I give thanks for my grandkids, Jasmine and James Coombs, who provided the beautiful illustrations.

A special thank you to the editor, Keivanna Thomas, for the time and dedication spent to make this book the best it could be. May the Lord continue to use your gifting for His glory.

Finally, thanks be to my Lord and Savior Jesus Christ, who has and continues to supply my every need according to His riches in Christ Jesus (Philippians 4:19).

Stay blessed!

PROTECTING THE NEIGHBOURHOOD

Soldiers Nigel, Henry, and Rafique went to a small village to protect the people living there. It was a dangerous area, and the people were very afraid to leave their homes. One night, as the soldiers were patrolling, they heard singing a far way off. They decided to follow the sound of the music, which they discovered was coming from a small church. When they arrived at the building, the people there explained that they were having a week of prayers and invited them to stay for the service.

The soldiers accepted the invitation. The sermon that night was about a prophet named Elijah, and how God provided bread for him when he was hungry. (1 Kings 17:4–6) Through this story, the pastor reminded everyone that God is a provider. The soldiers enjoyed the service so much that they made plans to attend the following night.

While the soldiers were attending the prayer meeting, their sergeant drove by the village. He did not see the soldiers at their station, and waited to confront them upon their return.

When Nigel, Henry and Rafique returned to their station, the Sergeant asked, "Where were you all?" The soldiers explained that they had visited the village prayer meeting.

Angrily, the sergeant shouted, "You went where? You were sent here to protect the people; instead, you went to a prayer meeting? Don't ever let that happen again!"

The following night, Soldier Rafique told the other two soldiers that he could not miss the prayer meeting that night. Soldiers Nigel and Henry responded, "Are you crazy? Are you really going to risk losing your job to go to a prayer meeting?" Rafique did not reply. Despite his friends' remarks, he chose to attend the prayer meeting that night.

When Rafique returned to the base, the sergeant was there waiting for him. The sergeant told Rafique that he had to choose between his job and the prayer meetings. Right then and there, Rafique decided to follow Jesus. He lost his job and did not receive pay for the hours he had worked.

Rafique had no money to pay his bills or to buy food. It was very difficult for him, but he never gave up. He remembered the first message he heard at the little church—the message that God is our provider and helper, on whom we can depend (Psalm 121:1–2). He prayed and asked God, "Please help me get a job."

The following night, Rafique went to the prayer meeting. After the service, he told the church members his story and they promised to help Rafique find a job. Two months later, one of the members got him a job in a factory. Rafique was so happy! Not only was he able to pay his bills and eat—he no longer had to walk around with a gun.

Boys and girls, remember to stand up for God—no matter what! He always has something better in store for you.

SPECIAL OFFERING

Shanola was a favourite little helper in Sabbath school. One Sabbath after lesson study, the teacher asked the class to bring a special offering for thirteenth Sabbath to help other children in the neighbourhood. Shanola, who did not have much herself, came up with an idea.

Shanola began to keep back part of her offering. Her mom noticed this and asked,

"Shanola, why are you holding back the Lord's offering?"

Shanola explained to her mom that Sister Teacher asked the class to bring a special offering for thirteenth Sabbath. Her mom was thrilled to know that even though Shanola had very little for herself, she showed such great concern about others.

That Sabbath morning, Shanola took her offering to her teacher. She was very happy to know that she could make a difference in the life of others.

Boys and girls, you are not too small to care for others. In doing so, you make Jesus happy. The Bible teaches us to show concern for others, and that when we give, blessings will come back to us in different ways.

Let's love one another, because Jesus loves all.

I Am Ashamed of You

When Little Peter was two years old, he fell down the stairs. As he fell, his dad jumped to save him and hurt his hip in the process. This left him walking with a limp.

Nevertheless, little Peter grew up in a loving home. All was well until he started going to school.

One day Peter's friend asked, "Why does your father have that funny walk?"

Peter was embarrassed.

The next day when Dad came to pick Peter up from school, Peter asked him to wait in the car. Without asking for an explanation, Peter's dad honored his request. For years, Peter continued to ask his dad to remain in the car when picking him up.

Then, when Peter was graduating from Junior School, he asked his dad not to attend.

"Why?" asked Dad. "What is your problem?"

Upset, Peter hung his head and replied, "My friends make fun of me because of the way you walk."

Dad was hurt. He asked Peter, "Are you ashamed of me?"

Then Dad explained to Peter that when Peter was two years old and fell down the stairs, he jumped to save him. "My limp is the result of a father saving his son," he said.

Peter was heartbroken. After crying for some time, he said, "Daddy, you are the best. From now on, I don't care what anyone says about you. You are my hero." He hugged his dad and said, "Thank God for a loving, caring father. I love you, Dad."

Boys and girls, let's remember to be grateful for our families and for all the people that take care of us.

KINDNESS

Pamela was very helpful in Sabbath school every week.

One particular Sabbath, the teacher spoke to the kids about the importance of being kind. She reminded them that Jesus wants them to treat each other nicely, as well as be obedient and respectful to adults. She then asked the class if anyone had helped someone or shared their snacks with anyone during the week.

Pamela shouted, "Yes, Miss!"

Later in private, another member of the class told the teacher that Pamela was not telling the truth about being kind or helpful, and that, outside of Sabbath school, Pamela was very mean.

The teacher wanted to discover the truth. She went to Pamela privately and asked her, "Are you sure you are telling the truth about being kind to others?"

"Yes, yes!" replied Pamela.

The teacher still wanted to make sure. One day, she disguised herself as an old homeless woman using shoes of different colors, old clothes, and an old hat that partially covered her face. The teacher then began to walk down the road Pamela took to school every day.

As Pamela walked to school, she saw the old woman struggling to cross the street. Annoyed, she sucked her teeth and walked past the lady. As Pamela walked away, the Sabbath school teacher straightened up, took off her disguise, and called her by name.

Pamela turned around. As she walked back to the old woman, she slowly began to recognize her Sabbath school teacher.

The teacher asked, "Is this how you show kindness, Pamela?" Shocked, Pamela remained speechless.

The teacher reminded Pamela that she must be kind to all people—even old people.

From that day on, Pamela was very careful with how she treated others.

Let's remember that Jesus loves us all (Psalm 145:17), and He wants us to treat all people with kindness and respect.

FINDING OUR WAY

Andrew and Judy were invited to church by their friend Yvonne, who was a church usher. After accepting her invitation, Andrew and Judy arrived at the church one Sabbath morning. The ushers greeted them with warm handshakes and smiling faces, then took them to their seats.

As they sat down, Andrew whispered to Judy, "Did you see the way the ushers invited people to be seated in sign language? Wow, that's cool!"

When it was time for prayer, Andrew and Judy noticed that the ushers did not kneel. Instead, they kept watchful eyes in case of emergencies. They stood ready to take a crying baby out of the sanctuary or lend a helping hand to someone who may feel unwell.

Judy and Andrew were so inspired that they wanted to become ushers too! They both decided to become members of the church and fulfill their desire to serve. Today, both Judy and Andrew are happily ushering and praising the Lord.

God used the ushers to show Andrew and Judy His love, and they gave their hearts to Jesus as a result. Boys and girls, God can use your smiling face and kind actions to show others His love too!

THANK GOD FOR A MOTHER'S PRAYER

David is the third child in a family of six siblings. Unlike David's brothers and sisters, who were loving, helpful, and kind to their mother, David would always get into trouble in school and at home. He was constantly being punished as a result of his actions. Eventually, even David's teacher gave up on him.

Tired of this behavior, David's mom started to wonder what else she could do.

Mother decided to stop punishing David. Instead, she began to pray for him and show him more love. Then, as mother became more attentive to David, the other children felt neglected and thought that Mother loved David more than them.

Mother explained to the children that she loved them all, but that she was trying to help David with his behavior. She then explained that she needed the other children's help to change David's ways. One of David's younger brothers came up with an idea. He began to write nice notes and place them in David's pockets, his shoes, and even under his placemat.

Every evening, Mother would close her bedroom door and pray for her family. As she knelt to pray, she would name her children one by one and ask God to take care of them. One evening, as Mother was on her knees praying, David stood just outside her bedroom door. He listened as his Mom called his name, asking the Lord to change him. She cried and said, "Please, Lord. I love him and I don't want to lose him. Please hear my plea."

David opened the door and saw Mother on her knees with tears running down her face. At that moment, David was transformed. He went to his room and wrote a letter to his mother, which said,

"Mother, I am sorry for the hurt I have caused you all these years. I love you, and I will cause you no more pain."

From that day on, everyone noticed a great change in David. When they asked him what made the difference, he replied, "Thank God for a mother's prayers."

Boys and girls, remember that your parents love you and are always praying for you.

THE SONG OF A CHILD MAKES A DIFFERENCE

Little Anna went with her dad to the nursing home to visit people that were sick.

When they arrived, the head nurse told them that Anna needed to be ten years or older to go in. Because Anna was too young, she would have to remain in the waiting room. As Dad went in, Anna stood by the window and looked at the people lying in their beds.

"Everyone looks so sad," Anna thought to herself. She wished she could do something to make them smile.

Anna decided that singing might help cheer the residents up. So Anna slipped through the side door and went from room to room, singing songs she learned in Sabbath school to the people in their beds.

Anna's dad found her singing and joined her. Then one of the residents, Mr. Lloyd, asked Anna where in the Bible he could read about the Sabbath. Though Anna explained that she was too young to read, Dad found Exodus 20:10 and read it to Mr. Lloyd.

The reading and singing put smiles on everyone's faces. The people in the nursing home were able to learn about the Sabbath and request Bible studies. Many of them eventually got baptized! Anna was happy she made a difference, and she thanked God.

Whether by singing, drawing or giving people a smiling face, you're never too young to make a difference in someone's day!

CHANGE THROUGH A DREAM

Keyon is a happy, loving little boy who always tries to encourage his friends to be obedient and kind to others.

One Sabbath day, Keyon noticed that his friend Andy did not put his offering in the offering basket, even though he had it with him. When Sabbath ended, Andy went to the store and bought snacks to share with his friends.

When Andy offered Keyon his snacks, Keyon asked, "Where did you get the money?"

Andy softly replied that he had spent his offering. Keyon refused the offered snacks, explaining to Andy that it was wrong of him to spend the Lord's money.

Andy responded, "It was only once; what's the big deal?"

That night, Andy had a strange dream. In the dream, he went up a hill and saw some beautiful flowers. As he leaned over to pick one, he heard a voice say, "All of these belong to Me." Andy looked around to see where the voice was coming from. Again, the voice spoke. "These flowers, this hill and everything in the universe is mine. Everything you have came from me."

Andy then realized that he was hearing the voice of God. The voice continued, "I love you, Andy, and I want you to trust Me to take care of you. Why did you spend your offering?"

Remorseful, Andy began to cry and said, "Please forgive me!"

The next morning, Andy told his parents about this dream. His mom asked him what he learned from the dream, and Andy shared that he would never withhold his offering again. Mom was happy and reminded Andy that we give our offering to God to show Him how much we love and trust Him. Andy agreed and was thankful that he had a friend in Keyon, who reminded him that everything belongs to the Lord.

Boys and girls, remember to trust Jesus with your offering!

UGLY GLASSES

Lisa is a happy eight-year-old with lots of friends in church and school.

One evening after dinner, Lisa told her mom that her eyes were hurting her. Mom suggested that Lisa go to bed early, hoping that her eyes would feel better in the morning.

Days later, however, Lisa's eyes did not feel any better. Mom took Lisa to see the eye doctor. After a few tests, the doctor told Lisa's mom that Lisa would need to wear glasses for about two to three years.

But when Lisa saw the glasses, she said, "Oh no! My friends will make fun of me!" Mom reminded Lisa that she would only need to wear the glasses for two to three years, and that she was beautiful no matter what.

The first day Lisa wore her glasses to school, her friends were surprised to see her new look. One of the students asked, "How long are you going to wear those ugly glasses?" Lisa began to cry and went home. Mom comforted Lisa and told her, "It's okay, Lisa; in a little while you will not need the glasses anymore."

Later on, Lisa's Mom said, "I know what we can do. Let's pray to Jesus. The Bible says that he is a healer (Matthew 4:23) and that he can't lie. Let's also pray that Jesus shows you how beautiful you are in His sight (Psalm 139:14), no matter what your classmates say."

Lisa returned to school. Five weeks later, another mean classmate taunted Lisa and said, "God is not answering your prayers." Lisa became discouraged, but a still, small voice continued to remind her that she was loved. Slowly, Lisa began to believe that she was beautiful, and that she would be healed in time. Every day before school, she would wake up and say to herself, "Jesus loves me. He made me special. He will take care of me."

After only ten months, Lisa's doctor gave her some good news: her eyes had improved, and she no longer needed to wear glasses! Lisa was very happy and thanked God for showing her how precious she was to Him.

Boys and girls, remind yourself every day that you are special to God, and that your help comes from Him (Psalms 121:1–2).

MISSIONARY FOR JESUS

Some Christian students attended a public school. They wore wristbands with the letters JWFA, which means "Jesus will forgive always."

One day during lunch time, a student named Tim walked over to the Christian students' table and asked them about their wrist bands. The non-Christian student had heard about Seventh-day Adventists and understood that S.D.A.

Christians wore no jewelry. Therefore, he was curious about the wristbands and wanted to know what the initials meant.

The Christian youths explained that the letters meant "Jesus will forgive always." They also explained that they were missionaries, who told other people about the love of Jesus and the forgiveness He offers to everyone. As Tim asked to be told more, one of the Christian youths, Rachel, took out a small Bible. She turned to John 15:12 and read it aloud: "This is my commandment, that you should love one another, as I have loved you." She then shared Psalm 32:1, which said, "Blessed is he whose transgression is forgiven." Rachel explained to Tim that God is love, and that when we come to Him with our sins, He forgives us.

Rachel also read Matthew 6:12, which encourages us to pray for forgiveness of our debts "as we forgive our debtors." She explained that when someone does something wrong to you over and over, you are called to forgive them.

Surprised, Tim asked, "How can you forgive someone who hurts you over and over?" Another Christian student turned to Phillipians 4:13, and told Tim that we "can do all things through Christ, who strengthens us."

The youth missionaries continued to talk to Tim and give Bible studies to the non-Christian students at their school. Because of their actions, two students gave their lives to Jesus Christ.

Boys and girls, you can tell other kids about Jesus wherever you are—even at school.

Trust in the Lord Always

The Williams were a happy Christian family. They enjoyed life and had many fun-filled times.

One day, Mrs. Williams went to the doctor for a simple blood test. Unfortunately, the result of the test was not good; the doctor discovered that Mrs. Williams had a rare disease. Six months later, Mrs. Williams died.

Both Mr. Williams and his son Allan were very sad.

Now a single parent, Mr. Williams wanted to set a good example for his son. He reminded Allan that anytime he felt sad, he could talk to Jesus about it. He encouraged him to find comfort in prayer.

After many years, Allan still felt an emptiness because of his mother's death. One day, he asked his dad if he would marry again.

Mr Williams replied, "No, son. It's me and you now; I just want to take care of you." From then on, Mr. Williams prayed that God would fill the void in his son's heart, and that, with God's help, Allan would learn to be happy again.

Allan grew up and went on to attend a great college. He thought about his mom often, and whenever he felt sad, he remembered his dad's advice and prayed. He recited his favorite verse from Matthew 5, which says, "Blessed are those who mourn, for they will be comforted."

Boys and girls, remember that Jesus hurts with you when you're sad. He's always there, and He always cares.

THE LITTLE PREACHER

Six-year-old Jimmy asked his pastor if he could preach one Sabbath morning. Delighted, the pastor asked little Jimmy what he wanted to preach about. Jimmy replied, "I will tell the people about the love of Jesus!"

The next Sabbath morning, the pastor announced to the church that a special speaker would be preaching that day. Jimmy came forward, and the church grew silent.

"I wonder what Jimmy will preach about," said one of the members.

Jimmy stood on the pulpit and said, "Good morning, church; let us pray!" He continued, "Jesus, please touch my lips. Amen!"

Then Jimmy began his sermon. "Church, the reason why we are suffering today is because of disobedience to God's Word. Jesus said that if we love Him, we will keep His commandments; therefore, the problem is love! We must love one another; if we cannot love the people we can see, how can we love Jesus, whom we cannot see?

"Romans 13:10 says that if we love, we will not hurt each other, and that love is the fulfilling of God's law. Furthermore, John 3:16 shows us that God is love! It says that God so loved the world that He gave His only Son, so that whoever believes in him will have eternal life.

"As I close, I'd like to say that I know I am little. But even though I am too small to have a job, I am big enough to tell of the love of Jesus. Jesus, help us to love and obey You. Amen!"

Like little Jimmy, you can share the love of God with anyone—even adults!

PRAYER IS THE ANSWER

One Monday evening, Eric and Joe were walking home from school. As they were talking about their progress in school, Eric offered thanks to God for helping them with their work. After the prayer, Joe asked Eric, "Why did you say thanks to God?" Eric explained that God is our helper in all things.

Joe asked Eric, "Are you one of those people who believe in fairy tales?"

Eric replied, "Not at all! God is real, and his promises are true!" Eric continued to talk about God and told Joe about Psalm 121:2, which says that our "help comes from the Lord."

"Ha-ha!" Joe laughed. "Can you see him?"

Eric replied, "No, but His Word tells me that He's everywhere, and that He takes care of me and you. He cares for everyone so much that he died to save the whole world."

Eric didn't want to argue with his friend. Instead, he suggested that Joe study the Word of God personally, to understand who God is. Joe got offended, but Eric simply smiled and explained to Joe that God loves him and wants to be close to Him.

Then, Eric prayed silently and asked God what to say next. He got an idea.

"You know Joe, I really love our friendship. Can we be friends forever?"

Joe looked at Eric in surprise. Then, after calming down, he decided to ask Eric more questions. The two continued to be friends, and Joe began to believe in God. Eventually, Joe learned how to pray and thanked God for the friendship between him and Eric

Remember that when you don't know what to say, Jesus will give you the answer!

BLESSING IN DISGUISE

Every Sunday morning, Ms. Judy goes for a walk. While walking one Sunday, she saw two boys, Ralph and Ron, playing at the street corner.

Ms. Judy approached the two boys and asked, "Would you kindly buy me some juice?"

Ralph and Ron looked at each other and began to go back and forth. "You go," said Ralph. "No, you go," Ron replied.

After a while, Ralph agreed to buy Ms. Judy the juice. She then thanked him and prayed that God would bless him.

The following Sunday, the boys saw Ms. Judy coming down the street again. "Oh, no," said Ron. "I wonder what she wants now." Ralph, however, was happy to greet Ms. Judy and asked her how her day was going.

After buying Ms. Judy's juice, Ralph returned to his friend. Ron asked Ralph, "Why do you help her? She does not smell too good." Ralph responded, "My parents told me to be especially helpful to older people. They're just like us—except they've lived a lot longer!"

You see, Ms. Judy lived alone; she had no family members to care for her as she got older. She was looking for someone to inherit her wealth upon her death, and, after seeing Ralph's kindness towards her, decided to give her wealth to him.

A few days later, Ms. Judy went for her usual walk. As she turned the corner, she saw one of Ralph's friends and gave them a letter to pass onto Ralph.

When Ralph received the letter, he curiously opened it. Inside was an invitation for Ralph and his parents to visit Ms. Judy at her home.

The next evening, Ralph and his parents drove to the address given by Ms. Judy. They pulled up to a nice, large house with pretty statues on the lawn. Ralph thought to himself, "*This can't be Ms. Judy's house, right?*" Still doubtful, Ralph walked up to the front door and rang the bell. Sure enough, Ms. Judy answered the door!

Once inside, Ms. Judy explained to Ralph's parents that Ralph had been very kind to her each time she asked for his help, and that he always treated her with respect.

With her lawyer present, Ms. Judy then said, "Because of Ralph's kindness, I would like to make him the sole heir to my wealth." Ralph listened in amazement.

Ralph's parents thanked God and Ms. Judy for the unexpected gift. Ralph was so happy! He even used a portion of the gift he received to bless a few of his friends, including Ron, who was in need of books and shoes.

Ralph remembered that each time he was kind to Ms. Judy, she would always exclaim, "God bless you!" Ralph then realized that it really pays to be kind.

Boys and girls, remember to show kindness to everyone! God loves a cheerful giver.

HONESTY

One day, Tommy's mother invited her friends to have lunch with them. Mother prepared all kinds of goodies. She even had Jell-o, fruits, and ice cream for dessert! Everything looked good.

While Tommy's mother was busy with meal preparations, Tommy decided that it would be a good time to help himself to some fruits. "*She's too busy to notice,*" he thought.

When it was time to set the table, however, Mother noticed something strange. What do you think she noticed? That's right; she noticed some fruit were missing.

"Tommy," Mother called. "Why did you take some fruits without asking?"

Tommy stood in shock. He did not have any time to blame anyone and thought to himself, *"I'm caught! She'll definitely give me a beating after everyone leaves."*

When dinner was over and the guests went home, Mother called Tommy. To Tommy's surprise, she had a big smile on her face. Mother asked Tommy to bring his Bible and come sit with her. Then she asked him to turn to Exodus 20:15 and read it aloud. Tommy read, "Thou shall not steal."

After Tommy read the scripture, Mom asked Tommy to write twenty-five lines of "I must not steal." Then she suggested they pray that Jesus would help Tommy to be honest.

Even though Tommy did not get a beating, he certainly learned his lesson that day. Later that night, before Tommy went to sleep, he prayed and said, "Jesus, thank you for your mercy! Help me to be honest always."

Boys and girls, remember that Jesus wants us to be truthful at all times.

THE POWER OF PRAYER

The James family was a very happy and playful bunch.

One day at work, Mr. James' supervisor told him that he could no longer have Saturdays off. Mr. James tried to explain that he could not work on the Sabbath, but the supervisor did not care.

Nevertheless, that Sabbath morning, Mr. James and his family went to church.

The next Monday morning, when Mr. James went to work, his supervisor reminded him that he no longer had Saturdays off. He then told Mr. James that he would have to decide between losing his job and working on the Sabbath.

Again, Mr. James explained the importance of the Sabbath. "Sir, the Sabbath is the Lord's, not mine (Exodus 20:8)," he replied.

"That's not my concern," the supervisor said. "Miss one more Saturday and you will be out of a job."

That evening at home, Mr. James told his wife what would happen if he refused to work on the Sabbath.

Mrs. James became worried. "Honey, if you work on Sabbath, God will understand," she said. "We have the mortgage to pay, the children's school fees to pay, and so many other bills. What will happen to our family if you lose your job?"

Mr. James replied, "We mustn't give up! Let us put our faith into action. Call the children; we will pray together and claim God's promises."

The family prayed for hours. After everyone went to sleep, Mr. James lay awake restless. He prayed and said, "Lord, help me to trust You."

When Mr. James reported to work the next day, he could not believe what he heard: a new management had taken over the business, and the new work days were Monday through Friday! All the workers had Saturdays off.

Mr. James shouted, "Thank you Jesus! Praise God!" From then on, he and his family always remembered the power of prayer.

The Bible tells us that when we ask Jesus for His help and believe that He can do it, He will always help us (Matthew 21:22). Let's remember to take all our problems to Jesus in prayer.

Returning Home

Maria is an exchange student from Italy. She spent many years in Venezuela studying and working hard; then, one day, she suffered a stroke. She spent many days in the hospital and recovered, but the stroke left her with a paralyzed hand.

Soon after recovering from the stroke, Maria decided to return to her family in Italy. However, she had not told them about her sickness, and didn't know how to bring it up. Then, she had an idea.

Maria called her family and told them that she planned to return home for a visit. She also told them that she would be accompanied by her friend Trisha. Excited, Maria's family agreed to the visit and did not ask any questions. Then Maria shared that her friend Trisha was ill, and as a result was unable to use her left hand. She would need help to prepare food, clean, and even take baths.

Maria's family began to hesitate. Although they did not refuse to have Trisha visit, they began to complain about the time and cost it would require for them to take care of her.

Disappointed, Maria told her family it was okay, and that Trisha would find another place to stay.

Some time passed, and Maria's family hadn't heard from her. This was because Maria returned to Italy without contacting them. Instead, she admitted herself into a home for people who are physically disabled.

Soon, Maria's family learned of her situation. They were very upset. Upon visiting her at the home, the family asked Maria why she did not inform them of her illness.

"We love you," they said. "Please come home."

Maria explained that she was very hurt by her family's response to her "friend's" disability, and that she was referring to herself when she spoke of Trisha. She then added that she chose to make the facility for people with disabilities her home. "The staff here is kind and helpful to me," she said. "To them, it doesn't matter whether I have money or not; their kindness towards me is unconditional."

You see, boys and girls, God's love is unconditional. He calls us to give without expecting anything in return. Let's pray that God will help us to love one another the way He loves us.

TOMMY'S BIRTHDAY

Tommy's 10th birthday was coming up, and his mom promised to throw him a party. Mom asked Tommy to write down the names of all the boys and girls in the neighbourhood. Knowing his parents had little money, Tommy was surprised at his mom's request. Nevertheless, he made the list and took it to his mom.

As his mom reviewed the list, she noticed that one name was missing.

Mom asked Tommy, "Why is Andre's name not on the list?"

"Mom, Andre won't come," Tommy replied. "His parents are well off."

"You don't know for sure, Tommy," mom replied. "Let's make sure to invite him." Tommy agreed and added Andre's name to the guest list.

The day of the party arrived, and guess who came? Andre!

At first, he was very shy as he did not have many friends. But once the day continued, Andre began to open up and talk to the other kids. Once the party ended, Andre invited all the boys and girls to visit his home to play sometime.

Andre thanked Tommy for inviting him that day, and for teaching him how to accept everyone.

Boys and girls, not all wealthy people are happy. 1 Samuel 16:7 says that while humans look on the outward appearance, God looks at the heart. Like Jesus, let's get to know one another for who we are on the inside, rather than what we can see on the outside.

The Unseen Lawyer

Pat and Kathy used to be the best of friends. Then one day, Pat accused Kathy of stealing her money.

Pat was so convinced that she said to Kathy, "If you return my money, I will forgive you."

Kathy started to laugh and said, "C'mon, Pat!" "You know I didn't take your money."

Angrily, Pat replied, "Okay! In that case, I'll see you in court."

After Pat filed a lawsuit against Kathy, Kathy's family promised to get her the best lawyer in town. But Kathy refused, saying, "I already have one."

The court date arrived, and Kathy was called to the witness stand. When the judge asked Kathy for her lawyer, she replied, "Sir, may I have a minute?"

After she whispered a prayer, she told the judge she was ready. Confused, the judge reminded Kathy that she could go to prison if she was found guilty, and asked again for her lawyer.

Kathy replied, "Judge, for the record, my God is my defense. Pat knows that I did not take her money. I speak the truth, and truth shall set me free."

After this strong testimony, the judge took a closer look at the lawsuit. Finding no solid evidence to support Pat's claim, he dismissed the case.

Kathy lifted her hands and publicly thanked God!

Why do you think the judge dismissed the case? Well, it was Kathy's faith in God! Rather than trusting in a human lawyer, she trusted God to be her defense.

Let's pray and ask God to increase our faith!

GOING CAMPING

The Charles family was preparing to go to camp. Mom told brothers Jimmy and Alex to pack their things quickly, or they would both stay home. But Jimmy and Allan loved to play, and they were slow to obey their mom's instructions. They thought to themselves, *"Mom will never know we didn't do as she asked."*

Mom knew that the boys were being disobedient. She waited until the day before camp was to begin, and decided to give them one more test.

That day, Mom told Jimmy and Alex that she had some last-minute shopping to do. She asked the boys to remain inside while she ran her errands and keep the back door closed. "Yes mom, we will," the boys replied. But as soon as they heard Mom drive off, they walked through the back of the house and went next door to their friend Peter's home.

What the boys did not know was that Mom had driven to the end of the driveway, parked, and walked back to the house. The back door was open and the boys were out on the neighbor's lawn.

Then mom got her camera and took pictures of the boys playing; they did not even notice the flash.

After playing, the boys returned home and Mom went to complete her shopping. When she returned, she asked, "Who went outside?"

Both boys said, "We stayed inside, mom! Just like you asked."

Mom replied, "Okay, I will ask again. Is there anything either of you want to tell me?"

Mom was hoping that the boys would be honest and tell her the truth. Sadly, the boys did not confess.

On the day of the camp, their Auntie Ann arrived. The boys were very happy to see her, and asked their mother if Auntie Ann would be going to camp with them.

Mom replied, "No, and neither are you boys. You both will go with her."

At first, the boys thought mom was joking and giggled to themselves. As they laughed, Mom showed them a picture of them playing outside. Immediately, Jimmy and Alex fell silent.

Mom felt sad knowing that the boys would not be going to camp, but she knew it was more important that they learn about honesty and obedience. The brothers apologized to their mom, promising to be obedient and to tell the truth always.

Boys and girls, remember that if you confess your sins, Jesus will forgive you!

ABOUT THE AUTHOR

Joan E. Calliste enjoys writing and telling children stories. She never imagined that this passion of hers would lead her to become a published author; she is truly grateful for every opportunity presented to her.

Today, she continues to enjoy writing, traveling, baking, shopping, and spending time with family and friends.

The author hopes that as you read this book, you will be inspired to become a better you.

"When God reveals His gift to you, I challenge you to accept it. Always remember that 'you can do all things through Christ who strengthens you (Philippians 4:13).'"

—Joan E. Calliste

CPSIA information can be obtained
at www.ICGtesting.com
Printed in the USA
LVHW072148140521
687443LV00019B/915